AF253259

ParaNormal Romance

D. Lee

ShadowGrams Publishing

ISBN: 978-0-578-47115-0 (Digital)
ISBN: 978-0-578-47583-7 (Paperback)

Library of Congress Card Catalog Number: 1-7414126241

The following is a work of fiction
with all resemblance to beings, past and present
being unintentional.

Dedication:

Mary: Hicks and Jane

Michael S. and Morgan McC

The Funky Karma crew (Las Cruces)

Sam S.

Michael C. and Nikita S.

Gene T.

Laura T.

Louisa T. Michael C.

The Calhoun, Logan and Pearson Families

Stephanie B.

Doug H.; Kristen and Billy A.

	Section II:	
Early,	**Disconnected:**	**Stories**
II: i		136
II: ii		142
II: iii		150
II: iv a		160
II: iv b		169
II: v		176
II: vi		182
II: vii		188
II: iix		194
II: ix		204
II: x		208
II: xi		210
II: xii		214
II: xiii		220

ParaNormal Valentine's Day

I: i

Were he to have had his druthers and the

appropriate access-key cards, he would most

certainly have arranged recourse to the

University's Time Machine and thereby

reduce the span of his life by several years

in order to bypass the rest of this terrible,

guaranteed to be more terrible even than the

stereotypically wrecked Friday February

13th: or the night where they who find

themselves to be normal if not passe, but are

none-the-less regarded by most of this world

as the font of Nightmares and the progenitor

of Shivers and Goosebumps; Monsters,

Freaks, Evil Beings: all are trying to get a

piece of that mid-February pie and hence:

Paranormal Romance Celebration Day was

born or rather hatched as it was as the

Petronius Arbiter of the whole bunch was -

so to say - a lizard person; The Lizard

Person, in fact: sadly the last of his kind (so

it felt) yet again February 13th and the bars

emptiness reminded him - relatively - of

his own emotional experience.

Hence the motivation for the time machine; middle

finger to the midpoint of his spectacles,

midpoint of spectacles back atop the bridge

of an over-oiled nose: just something else to

distract him away from cleaning the
laminated seating chart that their
anachronistically inclined establishment
continued to use, preparing to re-mark the
tables now that the various and
spontaneously explosive idiosyncrasies of
the first wave of diners had reached their
lowest possible point of energy and were
thus stable, but at best: only so unreliably.

Time had stopped for him; time being conscious
thought applied towards the studies which -
had this been a quiet night that he might
could have accomplished; had the hostess
shown up: even tonight: he might not have
had to walk everyone to their tables and
back.

For solace in such moments of frustration, he
would exit from The Real World - just a
scosche - and, directing that energy instead
toward his imagination which - thus
enhanced to a level of gain above that of his
perception of reality thus took its place,
precluding the need to a assuage hurt
feelings by instead always having ever -
been invulnerable and impervious to such
attack. Even if they were simple acts of
common courtesy which he was prone to
misinterpret as such turning them into -
with a touch of projection - deeply personal
attacks upon his integrity and overall sense
of proportion of himself in relation to others
(i.e. being unquestionably Superior, both
supporting and arguing against the facts of
reality).

And he was lonely too - he could not deign to let

this fact rise above the threshold value and

become conscious and thus lead to

compensate for the un-experiencing of his

feelings, he seethed as well as any lizard

person (who are notorious for holding

grudges stereotypically: something about

living underground, who knows) against and

toward all this happy couples and even the

poor single bastard at the bar - his boss just

(expletive deleted) him on principle: all

showing-off his Forehead Jewel: to the

mirror on the liquor shelf and no one else.

An icy cold stare toward the room where the

second wave of diners had already begun to

circle their meals, wheeling about in small

talk and induced romantic communication in

hushed tones (So as to better overhear the

18

strangers with whom one shared space)

proceeding in their Direction: even the

asexual Creatures got laid on February 13th:

One Day he would show them all…"

I: ii

Even now, several hours later, while waiting to be seated at this dump of a fine dining restaurant, the experiences of his morning obtruded into his awareness, the vile doctor standing in for the "Over it" Male Hostess, the impersonally ghoulish examination and bad news delivery room and the diagnosis that he had accidentally caught vampirism from his date; this diagnosis supplanted her presence in reality and for quite some time was all that could be handled. To make matters worse, the physician - the only physician available on such short notice and for such a strange enquiry, was his childhood pediatrician. Therefore he was, now a twenty-something-ish man, grossly oversized for the cartoon-bear and crayon-dinosaur decorated room, the child sized examination table forcing him, essentially, to curl into a ball atop the plateau for any semblance of comfort, or his legs would drag, stationary as he may be, upon the floor consequent of their two standard deviation away from the mean lengths.

He had not told her yet; not about the pinch that he felt that night or the two red marks which developed after and then switching to synthetic blood - thank God that he found a public health pamphlet *"Am I, a Vampyre,*

Mommy?" from which he was able to

extrapolate the necessary information - but

the doctor's ex-post sanguino diagnosis

rammed the Bolt of the obvious home into

the Stop of reality.

Throwing the chart to the tiny examination table,

the small sized, older-adult doctor of

children railed with utter delight at this

patient; he who had once given him so much

trouble, now back to ask for a diagnosis so

delightfully ironic as to justify a career

otherwise distended into unrecognizability

from the dreams which had inspired it;

hearing without cessation: children complain

about the pains of growing up and parents

complaining that the children were growing
pains, themselves...

" ... That's what you get for messing around with
the undead, Junior. Come on: she told you
she was a vampire and what - you are
surprised when you wake up with two
puncture wounds around your neck:
Diagnosis confirmed: Dumb Ass; Secondary
Diagnosis: Acute Vampirism; she is cute,
no?"

The aforementioned twin-wounds ached atop the
embarrassed blush that spread across his
body.

Back to reality in the crowded waiting room,
placing a hand on his date's back and trying

to see if her fangs were visible beneath her sculpture-smooth cheek skin. Anxiety continuously swept through his thought processes, disorganizing and discombobulating like so many tornadoes of thought: when could he tell her?; what should he say?; there was anger but he did his best to suppress it as one probably does not want to offend their vampire Creator on the day of their christening, or so one would think.

She smiled up toward his eyes and her eyes joining just a second later so as to watch him watch her and through appraising his appraisal did she allow herself the satisfaction of considering herself: "well turned-out" for the evening; he in a shambling business suit, and recently received a haircut and, at least, the suit was recently pressed: so it's wrinkles were fresh.

The fashionably disheveled werewolf waiter waltzed away with their drink orders and there being no easy way to begin, he attempted to blurt-out: " ...So I went to the doctor to have this abnormally large twin spider bite looked at - because there have been some complications, so to say, and the test came back positive for vampirism…".

"Attempted" was used as his date, who had been here before, as it were, and was no greenhorn blurter herself; her: "It Wasn't Me" tsunamied over his verbal ejaculation*
(* Let's reclaim this word from its sexy

dungeon in sexual euphemism land,

together!: they simultaneously ejaculated)

and he was there for a showdown; except,

scoring a weak-trump with: "But it had to

be you because I've never been with any

other vampires..."

She continued to flatly refuse and finally the

appetizers and aperitifs arrived only to be

trundled beneath the invisible boulder

pushed around the table with psychic force

only evidenceable by fury induced

photochromatic alterations within candlelit

eyes. Silence until, of course, they both try

to speak at the same time, leaving a

trainwreck of tense, misheard,

half-statements strewn now over their barely

picked-at entrees: and the werewolf waiter

Walth, he was really sweating it because time was money and he was on the hook to His Guy for "That" from the other night and hopefully, if the credit was still good, tonight - too - and then off to his casita with His Girl after his shift ended tonight; within his Lycan-Armored breastbone beat a heart which beat in two directions: off and on; beat off because he wanted to go Howl at the Moon, be a lone wolf: Los Lobos solo, as it were, but then now - even now - the desire to settle and get a Den and fill it with pups and reminders of their family eating sprees...

Needless to say a stressed couple doesn't tip-well and he's hustling away, quite quietly from the table as she began again: "I may have an eating disorder... "

He interrupted. "Don't say it's anorexia" .

She continued: " ... It's bulimia... ".

Again, rudely, he interrupts: "I've been used!"

She, rolling her eyes at his melodrama, as

vampirism was more of a lifestyle shift

nowadays, she had taken up telecommuting

during the day and taking… And moreover,

it was extremely un-fashionable for

vampires to drink Human Blood… She

realized:

"It's the Vambien: I started taking it to ease my

shift to sleeping during the day; I've been

sleep eating…".

"And now I'm Undead! "

" But looking great, too: there are upsides to

immortality, believe me".

Finally, with that, the ice-breaking around their

couplehood, the warmth of the evening

flowed within the interstices causing them to

flow apart and they themselves to flow

together over the table so to speak.

With a sly grin and a return to the entire

prerogative of the evening: "Conjugal coffin

visit?" he lets it float.

She: another sigh: "I... I... cannot tonight, it's A

Period Thing."

He, therefore stymied, but undeterred, could only

think to himself: "The concept of vampire

menstruation has yet to be tackled by

popular mass media."; nonetheless, he

persevered onward: "Maybe... It would

help."

"It will not, I assure you, help." Because her true

fear was actually that she was pregnant and

probably maybe it was the consequence of

an imbroglio not featuring, awkwardly, her

current lover who also possesses a much

better job and apartment and was also sitting

across from her at the table.

And we shall let this meal transition into

increasingly loaded Coffee service into

Desert presentation.

I: iii

(For Nikita Seeley and Michael Carrasco)

They were a good couple, if a little bit traditional

on the conservative side; his parents had

emigrated from Mexico, birthing him here,

in the states, whereas her family had

emigrated from a similar region so long

before as to render them virtually

indistinguishable from the normal

Americans, whose opinions he

unconsciously dreaded since, being a

first-generation immigrant, one finds

themselves pulled-in, at least, two directions at once, always - found falling between the balance point of traditional culture and that of the new world; as the first child, he was expected to integrate as completely as possible and had one been in and around this area during his youth, most certainly he could be seen translating anxious apologies from grateful parents to befuddled farm owners but the stereotype that hurt him the most - it was so obvious that his loving girlfriend - oh! Now fiance! Already predicted his grumblings and worked, prophylactically, to soothe them; She asks, gently:

"They have some really great vegetarian options, tonight; did you see them on the specials menu?" He nods an affirmation and continuing a sentence that happened at every restaurant that they'd ever been to: " ... It's kind of a racial stereotype to assume just because I am a Chupacabro, that I am going to order The Goat: And it never fails to offend me. They will try and offer a special plate of Frijoles, too…"

The sweetly patient fresh-fiance had triggered this conversation early in the meal for fear that the long simmering resentment would boil over at the waiter when he inevitably suggested tonight's Goat Dish. She felt, as much as she could, the sensation of displacement inherent to being born a foreigner in one's own country and did her best to salve this because underneath the resentments and compensatory strategies, she sensed the unique value that her one-day husband could and would impart to the world, especially through his promising Graduate Research into migratory cryptozoological feeding and mating patterns; a topic possibly motivated by the decision - the exigency - which forced his parents to first immigrate and then emigrate, despite having gained citizenship, to attend to seemingly ancient family business. The one-day-wife's strategy worked and to avoid the frustration of being Typecast, he prompted the ever increasingly disheveled Waiter for more information about vegetarian plates and the waiter did great until, apparently he was a little inebriated, thinking that he was asking on her behalf he offered a goat appetizer to the Chupacabro.

She, who still ate goat - ravenously - cut off her

date's reaction, specifying her own desire

for a small serving and then immediately

started his mind on a "go-to" positive

subject, conservation writing which revolves

around a cryptozoological animals.

Although an Avid Reader, despite the

disapprobation of his Fraternity Brothers, he

found himself forever in the debt of his

largely hapless - but respected - graduate

advisor for exposing his intellect to the

bright rays of a lost Aldo Leopold essay,

bemoaning the loss of creatures of whom

Empirical Science was unable to determine

if were in actual existence - or not. Writing

of his very same people, perhaps distant

relatives, some sixty years before the main

emigrations would occur, seeking less
devastated resources sources:

> "Now it's a darn shame that
> our ecological
> roommates are being
> shooed from the
> house before
> introductions can be
> made. While traveling
> through New Mexico
> and heading to hunt in
> the Gila, we came
> across a goat kill the
> likes of which I had
> never seen before: the
> animals were slurped
> right-dry, as if with a
> sanitary straw.
> Nevertheless -
> cowering in the

corner was a creature,

fat and happy, yet

scared and

apprehensive, as we

must have appeared

as mystical to it as it

appeared magical to

us. Of course

someone in our group

shot it, throwing his

corpse in the river for

good luck… "

That it was the desolation they were privy to

which motivated the founders of the

ecological movement to themselves move

mountains so as to educate the masses that

we live in a System as opposed to a merely

linear relationship in regards to our

environment this never failed to amaze him

and in his heart he knew that his perspective could help avoid further catastrophe. In fact, as part of his graduate program, he was tasked to the US military (he was sadly unable to tell his fiance about the best part of his job) to initiate, perform, and conclude environmental impact studies on animals and creatures and that asshole Bigfoot who no one believed existed yet were none less affected by United States military maneuvers in strange places.

Of course their meal, looking amazing, was delivered to the wrong table.

I: iv

Klink's and clatters of dishes and glasses; Small

     Talk blended homogeneously throughout the

     room: a sonic wave cresting away, toward

     the background always.

They ate listlessly, slurping or chewing their way -

     respectively - through the various courses

     saying little and remarking dryly upon those

rare probing attempts to interact, however stiffly, at their table while seated amongst the other Friday, February 13th revelers. Between the two: space, candlelight, their entrees and the always unspoken but nonetheless omnipresent wish: "Maybe tonight..." lingered most potently of all. One year had gone by since the formerly happy couple were last abducted, but that - he felt and knew she did also - the last session was largely pro-forma; lots of paperwork, there was a cake, everyone had their memory - however imperfectly - wiped, then they all hugged, shook hands, and they woke up back in bed. That quiet and big bed which they had shared for the year prior to that last abduction but even now he had loved her since the first abduction that he had been on and always hoped to be placed within a experimentally predesignated random assignment pairing with her. Already, in their initial charming interactions of furtive remarks while being strapped, unanesthetized, onto surgical tables and desperate, lunging attempts for normal human contact, only to be torn, arm-length by wrist joint to finger subsection apart; those brief moments really warmed him, however subconsciously. On the pretext of adjusting his chair the man, seemingly from his chair, attempted to kiss the woman, who - being on the other side of the table, presented a great target but a terrible goal.

Before the abductions he had been a motivational speaker; but there was something about the essentially random kidnappings - into Outer-Space or Kansas, he was never able to tell which - That shook and undermined his ability to warn children away from the horrors of drugs, partially because it was they to which he, himself, had turned in order to help integrate these shadow-experiences into his normal life; moreover, having not had drugs before the experience might be the most traumatic path, he was of the opinion now that although the perspective provided by the drugs was of immense value, that reality could ultimately trump any rival claim re: the superiority of utter-unbelievability; a thought he had grown to value as having the utmost salutary mental health benefit.

I: v

There was a house in New Orleans: where this

    Reptoid was born; hatched, rather.

My parents were on vacation at the time and took

    the effort to tote an incubator such that I can

    be seen struggling to life and awareness,

    breaking free from that shell, just before the

    stage which lay darkened but for a

    provocatively spot-lit foot; it's owner as to

    this day yet unknown. Destiny may be for

44

some a shooting star to chase after, to others it may be appear as a scooping net from which one is unable to escape. Some may feel a gentle pull - lifting them an inch above the ground as something else - the winds, perhaps, facilitates motion towards greatness: I felt ice cold hands atop my scaly cool-blooded shoulders the morning I was caught in bed with David Bowie and Mick Jagger both of whom were in my European Entourage at the time, in Paris before my "Darmstadt" concept album. On that morning I knew I had had - simply - enough, of everything and keeping this thought in the back of my mind while doing acid with Jim Morrison later on Sunset Strip (I thought the walk to Santa Monica was possible…) and he was telling me: 1. That his father, the Rear Admiral Morrison had willed him the family restaurant pre-posthumously, as a way of tricking him into acquiring responsibilities and, worse; 2. He really needed a seductive nickname to accompany the Annie Leibovitz, leather panted, photoshoot he was scheduled to possibly appear thereat somewhat later; I knew the solution for both - he could have my nickname The Lizard King, although I must note that in reality I am, in fact, less than a baron, in exchange for the restaurant that he was ashamed to be affiliated with in the first place. The deal was done, another sheet was quartered, divided, half-stored and half-consumed with the help of three topless women - L.A.!!! - I was able to use the phone booth to direct my attorney to perform the necessary task, my dealer to

prepare for the usual Tuesday night and I

asked Mr. Mojo Risin (He who was yet to be

he) to speak with less volume because all

five of us, in that phone booth, gyrating and

making calls: we were a Soft Parade.

Now, so many years later, my influence on the

Rock scene, multifarious and always

tactfully tacit, has faded from historical

perception. But I still have the royalty

checks and this bar to prove that I was really

there, gently tousling David B's Hair,

saying: "Rebel, Rebel: your hair is a mess."

or suggesting to Sweet Jimmy H. that he

seek a diagnosis for Bi-Polar Disorder.

Memories whirl by now, obscuring the reality of

this day, my own, the lone presence at the

bar, again, just doing the inventory -
looking over my glasses at a certain table to
indicate to the waitstaff representative where
their effort - The Hustle! - was most
urgently required.

But the memories! Locking Gary Numan into a car
with the help of Ian Curtis and Stephen
Morris; throwing John Bonham into a pool
before handing Keith Moon some horse
tranquilizers that became pretty famous later
on - when they had to pull a drummer from
the crowd, you know to finish the show and
everything - and I traded it all, in
ever-decreasing quantities, for the safety and
stability of this place - seeing as how the
typical life expectancy of my people is
around four hundred years, I find it flattering

that I am receiving reservations for meals 500 to 600 years from now. Mostly from the cryo execs and some style-forward vampires and Doctor Mummy at table 37, looking crisp, as usual, in Linen; would her date, the Monster of Frankenstein, as he preferred to be now called, be there with her five hundred years from today? If she does not wear out his batteries first! Into the mirror I looked with ease and poise; seeing the green and blue hues of my facial scales; the coal black impenetrable pools of my eyes; and I wish for one more trade - everything - all of this - for another Reptoid in L.A.

I used to have desires, they faded. Then went the standards and finally preferences were ejected as ballast to buoy my Icarusian romantic hopes. Today - today - today!: wait - how did a female Reptoid person get a barside seat and a drink with my having not been aware of it? Is she a mirage?

I: vi

The waiter was too stoned to notice him wince

    after he had commented upon the waiter's

    quick return with the drinks and the waiter

    thereafter saying: "Like magic" There was a

    wince because the couple of the table were,

    in fact: Magic, in the sense that they went to

    school to learn and trained practically as

    apprentices and journey people and until this

    morning, in his case, hence the wince: were

    licensed practitioners thereof; via some

    intrigues at the home office, just this

morning, he had lost his low-low-level bureaucratic position and had had his license revoked, precluding him from licit employment of magic for either Employment or Recreation and his lovely wife of three years had yet to be apprised of this information.

He took his time in stirring his drink, his wife kept half-looking up at him, hoping that he would half-look back so that she could full-look at him confidently, confident in the value of her affection transmission and his appreciation of it as it signified the receipt of a full look in return.
After cleaning out his desk he rode to public transit, in shock and not knowing really where to exit. He showed up at their

apartment with a box of stuff, he tucked it away in the garage hinting that it was a present perhaps for her - which was in the box, thankfully preserving his honesty - they got ready and she drove them to the restaurant, chatting amiably for both of them.

She was Nuevo-Witch and he dreaded, with grinding anxiety, sharing his financial concerns with her, it wasn't really fair - either way. To know or not know and there they sat, pondering the strange legal proceedings at the table next to them, in which an astonishing attractive woman removed an impossibly large legal document from somewhere in the seemingly negative space between her dress and body, which as they would overhear momentarily, was quite truly legendary and present it to her befuddled looking date, who was unprepared for the offer of the first, combined with the prospect of the second.

I: vii

Reading over the document, which he had been
handed after appetizers but before soup, an
inward sigh accompanied the understanding
of his intuition that his Paranormal
Valentine's Day date was, in fact, too good
to be true. They had met on a dating site
geared for mad scientists and their
assistants: "Sinister Plot" and although a few
emails were exchanged, and a phone call
had, he was somewhat surprised that she had

altered her appearance on the site-profile to look less attractive than she appeared, now. Although formally trained in Evil-Engineering, he recognized the contract to be a boilerplate "Soul in Exchange for" type document, and it appeared that he was being offered not only unlimited temporal wealth but also Helen Troy, his incendiarially-smoking hot date, who was an MD, JD, Ph.D, and LLC all rolled into one.

His date: returning from the bathroom, in which she witnessed a ghostly-spectacle - to say the least. He stands, pulls out her chair, re-scoots it beneath the table and meeting her eyes when seating himself, asking suavely as his hideously nerdish demeanor allowed: "So what's the catch?"

The room brightened with her smile and he lost

himself into her eyes: "There really is not a

catch; in fact one selling one's soul is

becoming blase amongst many

northeasterners; it's a painless pinprick

required to sign and if you would like we

could get married after dinner."

"Wait - we have to get married?"

"The devil is, true to form, highly traditional;

moreover, as marriage was an idea that

he/she/itself perpetuated upon the Earth,

there is a vested interest that it be kept

going."

"Is not marriage a holy sacrament?"

"The church is always stealing satanic ideas and

claiming them as original. Communion:

right, which is essentially ritual substitute

for the consumption of human flesh of one's

dead savior; old news: think the Greek mysteries. Yes, switching Bread and Wine into the mix was helpful since it lured the hungry populace into the game, Oh! Last Rites, right, here is another example; It's preferred to offer these as a final wish to the dying. Maybe they would like to see a pair of breasts before expiring, or a final Rock of Crack, the Last Wishes ritual beats the hell out of the Last Rites right."

"But, marriage: we just met; what if it does not work out?"

"First and foremost, I'm Helen Troy and I've married many, many men and have yet to experience a divorce. Second - do you think that Satan would dare break a contract?"

"I don't know that, you know; I have never had a girlfriend let alone a wife as attractive as yourself; what if you get bored or need to acquire someone else's soul?"

"Jesus - the report said you were insecure, but Jesus Christ; no one has ever considered that they would sell their soul and get screwed in the bargain; you are not dealing with angels here, who love to create falsehoods, since they thrive on problems but no: we are in it to win it."

"Is there an expiration date, attached to that contract?"

"Good question, it does in fact expire, tomorrow night, with your suicide."

"What can I trade for, like, maybe a make-out session?"

"Do you have any pets? I can actually take their souls now too…"

"No - but there is an all-night animal adoption

agency, just down the street... I've always

wanted a kitten…"

Thence - always at the wrong moment, their

Werewolf Waiter appeared and promptly

delivered the food of another table. It was a

vegetarian dish, but seem to be slated for the

Chupacabro couple, a couple of tables

down; Poor Walth: he instinctively retracted

from frat people.

I: iix

Because of the singular difficulties associated with

Intergalactic telephone routing, most

outer-space aliens eschew the difficulty of

phoning into fancy restaurants for

reservations and instead take their dates or

spouses to: "joints on the other side of town"

as one could say to a child with neither

offense nor prevarication. His date, an actual

human (whom he had met at work) had no

concern with the call and after their last Rendezvous, he only pretended to wipe her memory so as to facilitate the reservation process. Luckily, there had been a cancellation and they could get a seat. That was obviously not true as many seats were still there. He had a buddy cover his shift on the Mothership, he borrowed a saucer and picked her up wearing nothing as usual since aliens are naturally nudist and was delighted to see that she wore a similar costume, looking amazing, nonetheless and allthemorefor.

There had been a few stares as they walked up, mostly folk looking to see if her dress was actually invisible or merely forgotten at home, but she was right in asserting that this was a safe place for them to validate the ticket of their love, as every couple - it seems - represented a diverse or in fact non-existent, officially, population. He smiled at the servicemen vampires, sitting shoulder-to-shoulder at the fourtop; "They must still be in love"; he smiled at his date, who had tried to meet an alien for several years before they were set up on a blind abduction, as it were.

Then: Trouble; he points his face down and puts a hand to his brow, hoping not to be seen by a couple that he and had some of his friends had fixed up at work - as kind of a cruel experiment - only to watch - with muted horror- as the unnatural pairing set and took root, growing into the stunted plant of a subsequent relationship. His date wanted to

know what was going on, but for HIPAA
regulations, he was unable to disclose his
relationship with the two folks, so he said:
"Just someone from work; some people,
from work; that I want to avoid."

Thinking this was because of his shame for having
met her on an abduction, she began to fret
that she would never be good enough for his
friends; he knew this and also dreaded to
touch upon the ethical impropriety of their
own relationship, according to some of his
superiors, since it was only when he gazed
into her eyes, just before boring into them
with a laser drill, on the operating table, that
he knew love was to be involved in their fate
and future.

The couple that he was avoiding - he longed to
point out that it was a couple and not

another human female - but he could not -
were amongst the worst abductees he had
had the pleasure to run through the
experimental procedures as never, ever, ever
had they had trouble in dismissing
participants from the program, yet it seemed
that the ostensibly random and pointless
medical violence being perpetrated upon the
two gave their lives a meaning and point that
their prosaic existences previously had not
provided.

They were so clingy that the more senior alien
researchers devolved their
procedure-regimine upon him, as they felt it
would be a "good learning experience,"
always a frightful term, as when these two
were not trying to escape, they were

contaminating the carefully randomized treatment assignments. Finally he just got tired of it and, a little drunk, placed them into an experimental romance station itself made to look what the aliens believed to be the ultimate of romantic ensconcement on Earth: The Converted Westfalia Van.

They woke into a candlelit conversion van and essentially, also, within one-another's arms. This did not settle the two down and he worked ardently to have them thus removed from the trials which was eventually the case after the male of the couple learned how to play "their song" over the ship's PA system and proceeded to annoy his superiors to the verge of court-martials procedures.

Desperate to change his thoughts, and hopeful to

save his date, all the while wishing to

desperately avoid those two, he asked as

smoothly as possible: "How about we get

abducted tonight: just you and me."

She blushed, nodded in agreement and he

continued: "How about - right now?"

She nodded and he took her hand and rushed the

serving area just as recognition flashed in

the female abductees eyes a few tables

across.

I: ix

During the sudden departure of a couple, he was

otherwise more compelled to focus his

attention on his recognition of the strikingly

handsome lizard fellow, sitting at the bar,

but never from having seen him in person -

as he had - to his knowledge, never seen a

lizard person, in person, so maybe it was on

talk show or something. He looks like an

Oprah kind of fella. And his date was

returning to the table, he noticed finally the

lizard man making a move - relatively - on the lizard lady at the end of the bar.

His own date - ultimately the best direction of directing his attention - wore a close-fitting dress of red and black and there was nothing within him but the sensation of warm-astonishment; a sublimation resulting from the cement dread and worry inherent - for a year now - to his his soul - consequent being on the receiving end of one of her Smiles. The waiter, who had really "had it" by this point, just stood by the table staring at them, his eyes listlessly rolling about in their sockets. The specials indiscernibly pronounced, their drink orders forgotten before they had a chance to give the rest of their order, and slowly ever so slowly, was it

dawning on our poor werewolf server,
Walth, that he had just consumed a healthy
amount of Ketamine instead of a small
amount of Cocaine and he was here with
these people, right now, wondering if they
were closeted vampires (Coffined Vampires
- he chides himself, is the correct way of
saying that...) he realizes he had been
writing the drink order with the eraser of his
pencil, he takes a capped pen from his
pocket and without doffing the lid, he asked
for the two to repeat themselves, asking in
such an inebriated way and manner that the
stone sober couple sitting before him
themselves were concerned for their own
future temperance.

Summoning up the best of himself for a brief flash
of non-ennuied activity, the werewolf waiter

informs the tremulous table of their meal
choice, the wine they would most prefer,
and that they were already overjoyed by his
Spectacular, if but psychically detached,
Serving Style.

And the couple was all about psychic detachment,
in fact: they urgently sought more of it as a
ghoulish third wheel had attached itself to
the frame of their love bicycle. It has been
three years, to the day, that his ex-girlfriend
suicided as part of her online ghost
investigating psychic seance podcast and
YouTube, only, talk show; she had done so
to prove a point, regarding some pithy
comments section conflagration occurring
amongst the message boards of her Psychic
Friends Network or something and to prove

a point she suicided, and predictably to all but the person engaged in the action itself - via "Participation Mystique" - she lost her bet and consequently, failing to resurrect thereafter, therefore stood him up on the pre-arranged date of her slated return, as a ghost-date for ParaNormal Valentine's Day.

A year later, therefore: last year, some friends set him up with another girl; a new and a different woman than the one he is with now and on that PnV Day, even through the ever-lightening morasses of his trauma induced depression, something felt awry. For example he'd never seen a woman as graceful as that creature spill so many items on herself, especially on a white dress, no less; after the second bottle of wine cascaded down her neck and shoulders (it was white so as to remove the inexplicable red stain that had happened a few minutes before, a feat of pained logic possessed only by his late ex-girlfriend) that she asked to be taken home and he complied, hurriedly boxing the leftovers the gently wrapping his jacket around her sodden frame. Walking out the door, looking into the entrance mirror before every restaurant ever, he saw the patronizingly smiling face of his late, now ex-girlfriend - since he broke up with her for standing him up - gloating over the sunken shoulder of his date much as she did when finishing a crossword puzzle before he was able to do so way back in the day.

Tonight's date had received ample warning and she - herself- felt up to the challenge as she had recently read the book called: "Call the Dead Collect" and moreover to prepare they had attended, since they've been seeing each other for a few months anyway, some great practical sessions on dealing - at least- with the metaphorical ghost of others, with which they were optimistic about their probability for success if only because they were unaware of the challenges faced them this evening as the jealous, very bored, and entirely ignored - especially in the podcast world - Ghost Ex-Girlfriend was incensed that one of her dresses was now being worn by she, now at the table, mistakenly employed to boost the power of the countermeasures they had thought to employ, however naively of their lack of inevitable effect.

At the support meeting for spouses and significant others of recently deceased psychics they had met, hitting it off, and he had brought some of his girlfriend's old clothes to her thrift shop for Animals of divorce as it had been 30 months and he wanted to place notions that he would find her waiting for him outside his apartment, out of his mind as he changed the locks for a fear of the underworld may have corroded morals along with fleshy encapsulation, waiting to be let back into his home and his heart. Hence the dress, which was even more offensive to the lonely apparition, as it fit The New Girl much better than had ever, ever, fit she.

Moreover, this was entirely compounded by the lack of fashion-forward ghosts foreknowledge regarding the Dress Code of the Dead which specifies (I am taking this from Max Freedom Long, *The Secret Science Behind All Miracles)* that ghosts generally appear in the clothes they were last wearing when alive. So she - in her yoga pants and camisole athletic top dressed for death, forever leaving her insecure in the afterlife, aside from at the gym if she haunted every Tuesday and Thursday for the cute yoga teacher and she was a little upset with herself that she could not stand to see her ex move on but...

Although both felt aware of her presence, she intended to refrain from making a proper

appearance, however invisible, until much
later in the meal than last year, having
already learned how to affect credit card
terminals such that a perfectly good card and
account were recognized as being just the
opposite.

While gloating over the start of a lazy revenge
holiday, she traipsed around the room,
coming to a stop in front of a man in a
tracksuit, as she was unable to walk through
him like she had with the other occupants of
the room, she asked point-blank: "Are you a
ghost"; his response: "I do not believe in
ghosts."

He apologizes for being unable to believe in her,
either, if she was a ghost and sought to
politely excuse himself from the table where

he was loitering about earlier, maybe to do a

little haunting, maybe just to check and see

how the food was looking, coming out of the

kitchen. She had not interacted with anyone

besides humans, and then only in one

direction, since her death and perhaps this

had malformed her thoughts, a bit, already

malformed in the first place; she tagged

along after him, agreeing - so as to gain his

confidence - that they were definitely not -

under any circumstances, ghost-ghosts, but

since they were both dressed for the gym

and starved for companionship (she was

projecting this here, he was a loner in life

and death) why not hang out and get a

coffee, metaphorically and he apologized

but he had other places to be; she did not

have a chance to protest before he floated

around her and out into the steel cool

darkness of the February night.

Opportunities for therapeutic intervention for

ghosts is somewhat limited and she had yet

to process that it was her own hand that led

to her down his own path of ghostdom,

which - if she could haunt someone - it

would be to complain about being a ghost -

not to brag about how being how cool a

ghost was - which was the original

misapprehension that had been all the rage -

pent-up regarding this misfortunate

malunderstanding was piqued -an ice-pique-

by the horrific re-exposure to her own

desolate loneliness, the sensation running

back into a frostbitten limb or a damaged

nerve just to remind the soul what fire could

feel like, would feel like if properly applied
and this rage, thankfully she was at least in
cute yoga clothes, then vented through a
steam aperture warning all around of the
impending calamity as dishes and plates and
entrees and poor Walth go flying through
the air; those folk able to see this shade of a
shade were somewhat confused by the
rationale behind someone so attractive - for,
she was easy on the third-eyes - acting in
such a poorly-behaved manner. Two
women, filled with a Grace and Possessed of
a fluidity which belied their ostensible age
classifications and presumed tissue
ossification, rise from their table, nod to one
another grimly as they assured Walth,
however ambulatorily, that they would get
him down from there in just a few moments

and thankfully he was still so-so-gone that being suspended mid-air by a ghost while hoping to sneak outside for a smoke break so that this is very par for the course and these two older women, about which otherwise words fail to describe, save for the tender hands laid on the shoulder of this obviously hurt and priorly wounded Soul and the thankful resignation displayed by the ghost as she was led, such as a massive freighter sighs along after a tugboat, bumping and jarring after being stirred to motion and compelled to steer, into an awaiting restroom.

Whispers of soothing thoughts are shared into her ears by one of the women while the other, muttering something under her breath, turns to face the ghost, staring directly into her eyes: "Now if you do not start to behave Missy I will complete this exorcism I just started and you will flow into the Afterlife via the drain of this toilet."

She nodded in a sense. "Now", The Other Woman spoke saying: "Listen, you have had a break up and it hurts, we have all been there and, some are better than others but this one looks pretty bad for you but please know that we got up from our steaming platter of synthetic meat, to warmly remind you that proportion in response - if considered beforehand - is a habit befitting the grace of a gentlelady such as yourself. And to even more gently assert that your behavior in the dining room was askew from that." The young woman was ghost crying, which somehow preserved the untidiness of tear stained clothing, despite everything being unreal and it was just nice to be recognized as being a person, despite being a ghost she sighed, curtailing her sobs. The two women, their Good-Priestess / Bad-Witch routine fully exonerated, yet again, offer to seat the young ghost, starved for attention, at their own table, and the crowd - being fashion forward and therefore achingly tolerant - batted not an eye when a chair was pulled up and a place set for a non-visible entity. But everyone - especially the couple who had thoughtlessly brought their third wheel, was very relieved that the disturbance appeared to be over - if only for the moment.

Being about 1500 years old, between them, these corporeal but ghost-sensitive women saw fit to extend to the young spirit an invitation to "come home with them," as it were, and this was thankfully not presented in a creepy, tacitly sexual way, but in an affirming, overt way. "We've always wanted to be with a ghost, but never have been before…" (Not exactly true... But it works regularly). And in the end - a good day could be, would be, and was, indeed, had by this newly liberated spirit.

I: x

The grizzled Casual Fine-Dining manager did raise

    an eyebrow during the few moments of

    obtruding chaos when the spirit of

    ex-girlfriends past apparently "flipped the

    'F-out' ," but his pulse rate never rose; not

    since realizing who was sitting down the

    way from him; a lizard person Lady folk, all

    sitting by herself, listlessly stirring her drink

    then running a well painted claw across the

    paperback in a desultory gesture. The night

was otherwise going well, also, for that nothing extraordinary awful had happened; a laugh and a joke from stats class in night school: "Nothing more than two standard deviations away from the mean has been observed;" accept her, but - well - according to his definition of she, a 14 and a 10-point scale in which the average was 6 and a standard deviation is 1.5; it's significant, to say the least. And maybe it was a sign that he would allow himself to extend himself to someone new - or at least that it was still possible; a brief flashback of swimming out, his hard green body cutting against the muddy darkness of that awful river in Memphis which prevented him from saving Young Jeff Buckley's life.

Back in the moment - stirred, more circumrotationally than her drink. *Carpe momentum temporalis*, and all that jazz. First he is getting up from his chair, never failing to obtain is his the adjustment of the sweater over his shoulders and then suddenly from behind the bar, towel already in hand, he is offering this "Eye Apple" a fresh drink, on the house and she assents, without affirmation or outward agreement, and in receiving the cocktail from him chances to look up to the mirrored bar wall which faced her but for the photo of the gentleman who just served her this drink being kissed by - her eyes bulge out of her head somewhat - Janis Joplin, Joan Baez, and Mama Cass; his blush blush was readily visible, despite his scales deep, green-blue

luster and her own face, somewhat pale in
astonishment, makes the shape of words but
no sounds really comes out; across this wall
was a connect-the-dots of the rock and roll
world, since its inception and he sees this
and does his best to channel her
astonishment about his past into affection
for his present.

"That's the new house drink tonight - the sweet
tart heart. It's okay to choke, but give me a
signal you start to lose consciousness as I've
yet to lose a customer and it would be -
untoward, were I should do so tonight;
Thank You in advance."

Removing the aforementioned photo from the wall
he flips it down to her so casually that she

needs to straighten it to even make sense of it and while he is already going back to wiping the bar she sits on the edge of her seat as he says: "Rock and Roll History was made that night... " and she nearly fell out when nothing further was added. He fixed a drink for himself: Bulleit with three ice cubes and a stalk of celery. Having resumed his seat adjacent to the side of the woman, he begins.

Taking a parabolic route to the route of the conversation itself, he began to inquire as to if she was out tonight by herself, especially with the presence of invisible entities in the room, this question is prudent, regardless, however, always if but slowly inching towards the goal of ascertaining the current status of her heart.

"Oh!" She laughs and smile. "Funny you mention that; I... do not have one of those. It's best I bring this up early, especially as I feel a hint of warmth being exuded from your cool-blooded self towards me, but I'm a shape-shifter; my therapist suggested that I come out tonight having assumed the form of my inner self, but on the outside." There's a brief pause and a coy smile and she asks, without really needing to: "how did I do?"
"You display the noble attributes and attractive bearing of my mother without looking a thing like her; for which I shall be forever grateful. More importantly;" his eyes narrowed and she begins to learn why rock

stars loved him so much, *the good questions*:
"How do you feel, as a lizard person and a
lady?"

"The problem is - I do not feel much of anything,
anymore. I do not know when it stopped or
even if the sensation of experience I hold
dear as memory even actually existed."

He knew the type well. The denial of physical
experience to oneself is often The First
Resort for the satisfaction of the most
immediate and arbitrary of externally
inflicted desires. It is a useful expedient that
precludes the intervention of the body's
unconscious-conscious communication
safety mechanisms very tidily; until it's too
late to react and change one's behaviour.

Taking a moment to catch her eye, he performs

something akin to a Vaudeville magic trick,

so startling her that she laughs - sincerely -

with the vigor of a little girl and he

continues: "That - there, was a good laugh.

Did you feel that?"

"I could not help but feel it."

"But - exactly; which means, at least to me, and I

encourage you to stop me if this sounds

offensive or utterly incorrect, that you

should be - perhaps - more optimistic about

your prognosis than previously indicated as

you are still capable of feeling, but it seems

that your faculties to do so are blocked; my

guess is that it is because you are sensitive

and leave your house more than once a year,

causing you to suffer as all sensitive people

do in this modern world."

Breathlessly: "Yes."

"I bet that you were driven, partially - at least -

     to change shapes by the desire to modify the

     feeling of others, which inevitably allows

     for your own stasis, which is itself a

     desirable outcome in comparison to the

     unstable vicissitudes that fate's oscillations

     are known to oscillate between, several of

     which: I bet, have already gone against you

     by the time your feelings took the trunk-seat

     in relation to the emotional experience of

     others."

Quite amazed, and more than a little impressed,

     she was glad that she wore this body,

     tonight.

I: xi

Awkwardness attends some occasions inherently:

blind dates, executions, first days on the job.

If anyone noticed it, I believe that they

would find remorseless comfort in the

awkwardness experienced by a certain Mr.

X and a certain Ms. A, who, set up by

mutual friend experienced the strange

sensation of seeing someone for the first

time directly upon meeting that person - I

point this out as it implies a lot of data is

being absorbed quickly and it would be

natural for someone in such a situation -
especially as this situation contains a
remarkable caveat - to rely too heavily upon
heuristical thinking, instead of processing all
of the inbound information as it is,
algorithmically, hot off the press.

Now, this Mr. X, by way of profession was what
is conventionally referred to as a "Super
Hero" although he blushes somewhat at that
title (He is quick to say: "Bayerd Rustin was
a superhero, thank you.") but hero is the
appropriate appellation awarded to he, for
having had saved the day, professionally and
casually on that many occasions.

She, on the other hand, is not a tall woman who
nonetheless appeared to be quite tall,
possessing excellent posture and
horse-riding toned muscles with dark brown

hair, voluminously cascading down from her head over her neck and down past her shoulders, themselves bare to the night's cold in a dress worn specifically to allay her date's potential concerns - he is really sweet and kind of nervous - that this blind date may in fact be a trap, the the bare shoulders meant assure him that she was not in her costume. Explaining that to him he replies:

"That is quite considerate and thoughtful, thank you; it be somewhat inappropriate to reciprocate, the male fashions being what they are, but I assure you; that I am naked beneath these clothes, and I'm glad that you bring it up but would it be okay with you too maybe not talk about work - it's just, just that - I bet we know a lot of the same people

and I would rather than night remain
focused on us."

Appetizer in hand, heading towards mouth, she
vigorously nods in chewing agreement and
- using a tip that she drew from a
particularly helpful self-help book,
mentioned, after finishing the deglutenizing
of her buttered bread says: "You look very
nice in your suit." Which he appreciated,
despite that he was only wearing a sport coat
and jeans. And she did, in fact, look
particularly smashing, which he politely
addressed and before things could really get
going - the elephant in the room shit on the
table but they addressed it quickly, both
confessing sincerely - under the pain of
being 36 and 37 respectively and single

forever, otherwise, that this date was not part of a clever scheme on behalf of the hero, or dastardly plot if undertaken on behalf she. It was just a good old-fashioned fixer up. They were loosening, but both being work minded people, it was hard to relax - anyways - but with the added awareness of potentially very difficult tangents looming - albeit invisibly, they were none the less detectable, it was still too difficult to quite truly relax; to be frivolous. And perhaps frivolity has no place in the pragmatism underlying the serious world of modern romance, but both of these brave, lovely recipients of toxic waste powers, with a dash of evil on her mom's side - too - just wanted someone with whom to lay in in bed on Sunday morning, listening to NPR and laughing in concert.

While they are considering their entree choices, the casually finely dressed lizard man sitting at the bar, looking - romantically - at spreadsheets, waves to her and shortly thereafter a bottle of Laurent-Perrier champagne is delivered, with a wink from the lizard fellow who turns his back on the proceedings to better watch them in the bar's mirrored-wall.

Mr. X raises a quizzical eyebrow and she laughed, saying it was an old friend, in fact she had studied under the fellow while he held an adjunct post at the evil undergraduate school which she attended, receiving her degree in Evil-Accounting, she thought it was a multivariate statistics class, but could not remember, nonetheless, he had proven an incidental mentor of sorts and she did not know that he would be here but: "Thank you, Yes, cheers for the champagne!"

It was exactly what was needed, benevolent intervention from a charitable third-party deity who recognized that this couple could, Couple, if only: "They loosen up just a touch." Other tables looked on somewhat jealously that these two were still strangers to one another, seeing how easy it was to laugh - spontaneously in the company of another simply because of a champagne cork pop and the couple began to lean closer to one another across the table, early courses largely disregarded in favor of the interaction, itself. Faces drew even closer to one another over the table, getting close enough see candle fire light reflections in the pupils of one another. At this point he fully noticed her otherwise extremely nondescript cybernetic eye emplacement, and it glowed with a hint of orange in the pupil, before the fires light.

"Tiger's eye!" he blurts out.

Somewhat sensitive to the fact that he had been staring a for a few moments before mentioning something about an eye, she became somewhat defensive but he quickly reached out to gently touch her hands so as to allay her anxieties, while explaining that the mixture of colors in her artificial eye reminded him of the synthetic mineral, Cat's Eye or Tiger's Eye, as some people call it, which at least in his memory was a similar color. She was really sensitive about her eye, and was stunned that it's reality was addressed by an actually-attractive man in such a tasteful manner. Moreover, she looked to see his hands holding hers, and she liked the support, despite ordinarily disdaining physical contact with others.

Her face rose to meet his, smiling, a hint of a tear suggesting to Mr. X that he was able to say something correct finally, first date fears causing every statement to sound like the worst possible option. "Oh Jesus!", he hopes. She knowingly read his mind and said "Thank you, yes I know what you mean; that was really gentle of you to say."

"It's honest!"

She smiled, her hand now sneaking around to hold

his, gently squeezing it, saying: "I know,

that's why I did not vaporize you where you

sit with its laser."

"I'm impervious to lasers anyway." he mentioned,

his false nonchalance exactly complimentary

to her sense of humor.

I: xii

The candle's globular patterns of flickering

luminescence cast the couple now in a

flatteringly dim light, now in an even more

flattering darkness; silence washed - warmly

- between them as a "moment" was just

mutually experienced; a moment wherein an

attribute of herself which was as utterly

unimportant as it was inherently

apprehension inducing brought, instead, the

utmost of salutary comfort to he who -

although it did not really show - had once suffered a wound which he felt, until just then, that no psychic salve could solve; to wit, let us recapitulate the last few moments.

Drinks arrived and in the waiter's wake a hush fell into the space where nervous Small Talk would exist otherwise; the vacuum created by the touch of self-conscious embarrassment; resulting from being frankly, flatteringly, paid court by an actual gentleman suitor and he, saying:

"Ordinarily candles at the table would cause me significant distress, quite possibly triggering any number of awful panic responses, but you: there, is all I can see."

Always the therapist, she asks: "And why would a soft light cause you such concern?"

He was quiet and ordinarily would have remained so but the gentleness with which the question was posed allowed him, even then, to start healing in relation to: " ... Being chased by villagers and Towns Folk with fire and various items of farm and garden utility; the usual Monster Sob Story..." And he tried to play it off.

She was quick to point out that he was not a monster per se but that this was merely an unfortunate nominalising appellation. For example, she was a "Mummy" yet never having been married or even her having had children. The hidden dirt of stereotypes always lurk in the supposedly hygienic

crevices of labels and even - if not most
especially - from technical names.
He loves her over gustatory response to
inappropriate stimuli and here, although it
hurt a little bit, was a prime example of she,
despite being Undead, really trying to live
life to the fullest: she laughed in his face,
loudly.

He blanches, she reaches out energetically, leaning
forward to say: "That's just because you are
young! Sure, that used to hurt my feelings
too, but I mean - look at it this way; when
that first started happening were you not
inclined to Revenge yourself upon the
villagers etc for the hurt done on to you?"
"Yeah," defensively, "But that is natural? Right?"

Softly, certainly, she responds: "Yes, it is
something that we have all resorted to, in
times of anguished abandonment; frightened
and alone - terrified by threats to ourselves
and our bodies; but the true criterion and
root of my question is: 'would you respond
like that now, after some...' - she states this
delicately - '...decades of reflection?' "

"Yeah - no: you are right. Nowadays it is much
easier for me to un-panic a mob and my
lawyer or agent or accountant can fix about
everything that I am unable to handle."

Here, now, the aforementioned appreciative
silence, the before referenced gazes of
adoration exchanged while timorous
thoughts of the future themselves sparked

and ignited in their hearts, minds, and nether regions.

Other tables, those occupied by the more

"seasoned" couples, so to speak, appeared at

first glance to be suffering mightily, but

upon closer inspection may conjugally

participate within a vastly more complex

ecosystem of factors affecting: pleasure,

fear, satisfaction and the like; for example,

Mister Swamp Monster, of good American

Stock - e.g. Not The Bayou Swamp

Monsters, thank you - and his wife of 12

Years, the Lady Bog monster. This title, however illegitimate, is much easier than attempting to describe the family dynamics of the "Bog-Windsor genealogy and titular Holdings; thus "Lady" it was.

Here it is, the corporately maintained corporeal holiday, and Mr Swamp Monster grumbled onward; at first he had desperately sought to change seating times because something - always something - needed to be filed before he could leave the Law Block of Downtown and now: utter disaster.

Speaking At his wife instead of: "To" or "With" her, the avalanche picks up momentum: "How could they run out of fish on Paranormal Valentine's Day? Heaven forbid they

transfer my meal request with my
reservation... I am a swamp monster and this
denial of fish has a "Specist" tinge to it…"

But - and so subtle the untrained eye would never
catch the true weight of such a delicate
maneuvering, the Lady Bog Monster, with
the finality of a leaf falling to float into
quicksand, her hand came to be atop his own
and soothed the pugnaciously truculent
outburst and reminded him that without even
saying a word: "Why it was all worth it,
after all."

And yes - he appreciated the reminder, but, only
later and quietly. Nonetheless thankful
always for the perspicuity of his wife.

I: xiv

A lesser known fact as to they who exhibit a

deficiency of refractive capacities, such that

light passes through, instead of bouncing off

of them - The Invisible - is a cruel epithet

applied to this condition and this lesser

known fact is that invisible people are - see

how deeply the label of Oppression

permeates that I am so afflicted by the

necessity of its application and for this I

apologize - they are - as a rule:

self-conscious to the point of paralysis in

certain situations, often times with more

than one invisible person becoming so transfixed, such that a room could become - to the visible party of the one individual within it - nonetheless, so crowded as to promulgate a feeling of intense awkwardness and dread, to a certain extent here is lesser known fact #2 - that on occasion prostheses are worn such that one may receive a confident coffee order from a beard floating before them, holding a copy of the New York Review of Books or an amazing $1,000 pair of shoes just may walk by, by themselves.

At the combination of the two, two-tops, making a table for four: the beard sat catty-corner from the amazing pair of shoes, with a pleasant, somewhat overtly middle western female sitting across from the former and her male counterpart sitting across from the latter, enjoyed the online service facilitated date small talk but the invisible members, even at the stage of the cocktail course, were wondering if, perhaps, there has been a mistake and instead it would be better to rearrange their place cards, as it were. But it was as yet unspoken - primarily as the beard struggled to determine if the shoes were interested in him from their attitudinal direction of toe-points.

These suspiciously overt middle westerners knew - on the other hand, primarily, via the extension of the hive mind complex that they - as Extra-Illegal-Alien infiltrators they themselves had access to - they knew

that this date and the seating arrangement
was highly desired as the Extra-Illegal-Alien
Dating Site that the invisible couple had
unwittingly joined was more interested in
finding and arranging for the acquisition of
innovative genetic material for the
Extra-Illegal-aliens to then exfiltrate -
despite being infiltrators themselves - back
to The Mothership for the extrapolation and
integration of the appropriated material.
Invisibility seemed to be the perfect addition to the
extra illegal alien toolkit as - if they could
not be seen, perhaps it would be more able
to seamlessly integrate into American
culture, Xeno-XenoPhobic as it is: so that
the lessons and the wisdom of their cultures
may be shared in fulfillment of the alien
commandment to missionarize the populace

or to, that failing, put them to the sword;

plus they wanted to pay taxes, too they felt it

was their responsibility since there were

living in this country, now.

The invisible couple - despite being two

individuals at this point - did their best to

attribute any of the numerous conversational

oddities to the middle westerness of the two,

while the Extra-Illegal Alien infiltrators

struggled to bring to bear any of the negging

strategies they ordinarily employ to seduce

their donors. They had read: *The Game*. No

result to: "Have you lost weight?" The

female middle Westerner ostensibly, at least,

was able to elicit a response with: "Is that a

new beard?" as it in fact it was.

Appetizers arrived and The Shoes share an

anecdote such that the table gets to laughing

and the Invisibles man's hand is deftly

caressed by the Middle Westerner female

and he gasps with a sudden retraction of his

hand because it appears, the only way that

was possible, was if they, she rather could

have seen his hand beforehand: "cyborgs";

he reasoned, "goddamn cyborgs." He

needed to signal The Shoes as to the peril

that awaited them at the proposed

destination of a name brand Combined

Romance Suite, an offer floated daringly

early in the meal - in fact during the order,

in front of the waiter who thought it was he

who is being invited. The Beard worried

however, because he'd always vowed never

to marry a woman who looked like his

mother yet - there she was: dark red heels and all. He laughed and thought of the story of the tourist group who died because one person, being pulled into the quick-muck type of mud, shouted: "It's giving me a great deep tissue massage and Nutrafying my skin simultaneously!!!" Knowing that this would lead people into the muck where his screams for assistance hitherto caused not a muscle to budge. The only ones who survived were they who are unable to fit into the space of the pool after it being filled to capacity by the initially responding tourists and the victim who was unable to escape no less.

I: xv

One table over - fate would have it, a cyborg was

sitting with his human date, yet while he

worked to downplay his cybernetic

architecture she ostentatiously displayed

artificial robotic enhancements, almost

gaudily, with her face laser shining into the

wine glasses or directly at the breast of

whomever she was judging or attempting to

have judge her at that moment. Despite their

proximity to the bog monsters - or perhaps

because of it, they, nonetheless, were a chipper couple, both warm and buoyant, but only he was able to see the invisible couple at the next table: "They're always naked, as people", he marveled - but he knew it was impolite to stare for they were unfailingly shy; knowing this from having served with several invisible gentleman in the rather unique and explicitly non-existent unit of the Army that allowed him the chance to utilize his gifts as a second generation cyborg, without feeling the stigma associated with such a transition, in proper society. In fact the chance to be valued and appreciated for his differences was offered: and deathclaws, to which he had said: 'Hell Yes.' Trudy - his date - had adopted a robot name that he found difficult to pronounce as it was in

Machine Code; they had met at a mixer at

of sorts, she had only started - gently -

exploring the world of superficial robotics,

the laser brought out her eyes - she

explained to him, who needed his own

Hardware after his cyborg parents fell atop

him one day in a hideous flag football

accident, and has always kinda wished for

the normal life his own life was un--allowed.

Trudy - his date - was deeply attracted and

he was constantly surprised with the endless

delight she exhibited in even the most

mundane of his cybernetics; loving to flip

the latches which led through various

hatches to his illuminated, pulsing inner

processes. She joked that she was looking

for his soul and figured it was near the

digestive modules - although he could not,

he did feel her subtle touch through his
titanium inner bits and he told her,
whispering so as to not aggravate the
auditory enhancer she wore in her ear - that
she reflected beautifully in the candle light
and with his mechanical deathclaw reached
out for her hand, holding it with a gentleness
provided by the inhibitory potentials of love,
he transmitted a gentle electric shock to her
hand and she felt it - nodding in agreement -
her ocular laser misting a little bit with the
tears of being too happy.

I: xvi

Kathy - our midnight haired vampiress - wore her
blood red dress in the manner in which it
was intended: as an afterthought provided to
the handful of Mortals who may have
complained about being in the presence of
such an amazing figure and her old friend,
Annannethia, she of the short blonde hair
and rail-thin, well-muscled physique, wore
her own shift in the manner of a portable
altar - always lifting and exalting she being
framed within. Their husbands, being no

spring chickens to Fashion themselves, both wore black suits - not tuxedos! - with the red accoutrement alleging their Heritage and the festive day. They had all known one another for thousands of years and after their numerous talks, the wives gained the temerity to bring up the idea of some sort of group sexual adventure with their husbands. It was somewhat Darkly alluded to first, but as the drinks gained more of a whole the topic was more forcefully broached and Drac frankly offered: "Oh like when Vlad and I go on our fishing trips?" There was a moment of silence and perhaps one of the wives ventured a slow "Yessss…" And they will cool and it was discussed at that relations were potentially inherently masculine, being between two dudes, and

that no one could ever impune the
heterosexuality of two dudes who -
between them staked like 30,000 peasants in
a two-year span alone, together.

"Except Freud!" The wives blurted out, this being
their favorite personal retort to their
husbands perpetual bragging about their
more savage youthful exploits. That and
basketball - the watching thereof - was
how they spend their time now.

To a castle - thence - somewhere in the valley or
perhaps near Topanga Canyon, the couples
warmly repaired to learn about themselves
through others and others through
themselves. This year's paranormal
Valentine's Day now being completed, our

poor host did not get out early to do homework because Walth skipped out on this side duties. The rest the rest is up for One's Own Heart to suggest the outcomes. Provided they be, my only request - less than predictable but self-effacing and uplifting nonetheless.

-FIN

Section II:

Early, Disconnected: Stories

She strode out and farther away into the newly

     fallen night, leaving the moment of -

something - to reverberate into

     incomprehension behind his furrowed,

pronounced brow.

Shaggy red hair holding the day's light long

     enough to glow in its absence; maybe even

the quantity of reflective photons sufficient

     to stimulate enough of one's Peripheral

Retinal Rod cells so as to create a sensation

of something: unusual - itself then
developing into the perception of a
Sasquatch which, thereupon actual and
literal cascades of neurotransmitters leads to
the apprehension of Certain Doom, spoken
aloud: "...could it be that I and She are soon
to be: a 'We'?"

A sigh of warm resignation to the undertow known
as "Mating Season" sonically-slid beneath
the rip and shred of high-quality tent nylon
and otherwise unblemished Virgin
Gore-Tex; that evening's song in the 'key of
terror' offered a continuation of the melody
started during a fortuitous juncture in space
and time - way back when - where some
contrived reason led the two - then -
strangers to innocuously begin to enjoy one

another's "just-friends" presence through the shared hobby of startling long distance through-hikers too fatigued to differentiate reality from its opposite.

"At first all we did was laugh and each encounter involved progressively less logistical effort until that, rather: This fateful day…" in which tension sizzled through the air and static electricity leapt from his outstretched, pleading, furry fingers: "I just did not know that we had officially made plans; maybe we should talk to one another about the others role in one's plans before criticizing them for failing to meet obligatory standards."

Screams punctuated by confused expletives staccatoed through his linguistic attention and into static chaos thereafter; it seemed that his friends, teasing him for his lack of presence on the scene, the changes to his grooming patterns; his recent shift to vegan hikers to match hers; it seems that they have exiled themselves, being good friends, to singledom to avoid her dominant menstrual influences: all of these factors sum to equal that they were dating but did not know it yet.

In the distance, sticks ablaze, he sighs again and lumbers toward the shifting shadows of red, white, yellow, and orange. How odd that natural behavior - e.g. arriving at a mate based on the shared enjoyment in life experiences - felt so unnatural.

Grabbing the torn remnants of a brand new technical sweater and dragging the beatifically emaciated through-hiker towards him, a convulsion of moral relativity shook the perennial desire to avoid labeling of a dreamed-after-happening - as such - so as to avoid the inevitable degradation occasioned by actualization.

II: ii

The modern Conference Center in a trendy

Southwestern Town consisted - it seemed to

him - of an interstice of crystalline

escalators, further transienting the already

transient, albeit iterently, convention-goers,

in terms of space and time: from themselves

and others.

There she was, escalating up from the depths of the

dark-sealed parking garage, carrying a

poster-tube and being utterly oblivious to the

world around her; not grasping that her

gravity was such to significantly-affect the
trajectories and orbits of those bodies she
even distantly effected(sic).

His own poster tube under his arm, his own
escalator drawing him in a different
direction: a public sigh and a private
visualization that their relationship was such
that she was always out to lunch and he
forever chasing afterward shouting: "But
you ordered delivery!"

They had met at a conference, such as this, while
he was finishing his Doctorate and she was
revolving into a prestigious, if but shadowy,
second post-doctorate in Transylvania. She
was to work with the: "The Learned Old"
to finally blot out the Sun but consequent

upon their meeting, thence, and an incidentally made, pithy comment, which affected her such that, you know - especially after a couple of mixed synthetic blood drinks (and while remembering this he wished to the god that his own existence negated, to -now- take back the remark that he -then- said in the height of his Social Science Doctoral Hubris) as he magnanimously queried into the air: "Wouldn't it be kinda, like, bad, for those beings who do require light, if we were to blot out The Sun?"

And although her response was sporting in it's ironic utilization of Malthusian theory to reflect that as they, being vampires, no longer preyed upon that humans, another form of population control must, therefore, be employed, with Utter Darkness being both the most economical and maximally facilitative to be vampire lifestyle itself, nonetheless; it was, as he later found out, boilerplate shit lifted directly off her application to that second post-doctorate which upon her recycling at that point in time that he hoped maybe mildly warmed by his presence - first sounded hollow and off-key in comparison to the richer tone of a harmonically equanimeous balance in the vampire ecosystem with their former food source, now left to multiply unfettered and hideously inflated with chemicals rumored to be, toxic - at the least - to vampires themselves, despite their immortality.

To these ends she, now 10 years later, intended to
present her findings and subsequent
refinements of her beliefs in a seminar that
he, however happily or non-, was first slated
to attend but upon the unforeseen
wood-staking of the moderator, his own
Undergraduate Mentor whose thoughts and
beliefs provided the rigidly flexible
substructure of his own Foundational
Beliefs, which therefore professionally
devolved to him to fill in, consequent of the
tragedy.

"If only he'd been wearing a shirt of foil:
aluminum or tin or something; it wasn't a
big stake, at all, and it may have even been
accidental... " Droned the female who had
cohabitated with his late-mentor in a manner

below that of spousal and above that of chaste, into the telephone, obviously blown on Vampanxiolytic pills, to tell him of the sad news: that he was selected to be replacement moderator, and also that his mentor was staked while virulently defending the right of werewolves to receive state sponsored silver bullets if they so wish to pursue euthanasia to end their own immortality. He died while decrying the so-called back-alley methods of self-termination werewolves were then being forced to seek, with the inhumane bullets of the basest quality silver, final relief of the Eternal Torment of their own un-depilatable experience.

"It was a damn Chopstick." the semi-widow snorted into her corded phone: " ... He would have loved that - after five thousand years of a powerful and thought driven life, a clumsy undergrad could manage to Harpoon him, all out of the black and whatnot."

His own studies had drifted away from those of his undergraduate mentor's and were now related to the field: "Humans who wanted to transition to vampire but were unable to do so" - as distant from her early humanist influences as the distance grown between them; another failure of his mouth occurred right between right around then too, something was said like: "...you are the glass slipper in to whom I'm destined to place my

foot."

II: iii

Brains: brains; brains.

Life after the apocalypse was - but for a few key

differences - rather similar to the times

before it. Humans have an inertia about

them, now - in fact - even when dead they

remain alive; aside from some-certain

dietary limitations inherent to optimally

subsisting upon the neural tissue of the

living-living, and the conversational fixation
it implied, most everything was pretty much
the same.

We had agreed to meet at The Art Show and, you
know, if we hit it off, go and derive
nourishment or perhaps find a liquid to pass
through our faces, my memory displaying
the image of her remaining lip thence
curling upwards: the coquet! One would
think that the state of being deceased would
somehow preclude awkwardness from early
potential romantic interactions, being that
the only audible sound capable of being
produced by all of the living - deceased is,
horribile dictu: "Brains."

If anything, I'm compelled to be a better listener,
and compensate for my articulatory-deficit
thereby. Yet, that human inertia lurches
forward through all aspects of this upgraded
Humanity, I still fear-about our conversation
tonight and how the interface between our
disinterred faces may-be if the space
between them evacuates atmosphere and a
vacuum thus occasioned?

"Brains." she said, shambling up the art gallery's
ramp.

"Brains. " I said back - thinking, just then, to
mention that I have been thinking about a
few of the ideas she had shared when we
met at a mutual friend's party and... "Brains
- brains; brains."

This is where the improved listening has come to better define me as a potential: "Late" - e.g. Since "Mate" had gone the way of the Dodo, "Late" is the current fashionable term for the long-term Undead-Partner.

The exhibit was somewhat stale in that we all have seen Blood and Guts and Entrails and Bile and every other human mess producing fluid dragged across every medium by now - so the concept of that that's like always - but now with an overlay of more Blood and Guts and Entrails Etc being projected thereupon, an: "Immersive Aesthetic Slaughter", was what she had called the style, after first saying: "...since, when chasing down a pack of seething, frothing humans, who has the time to create, anyway?"

"Brains": She said back, the part of her left arm with attached cutaneous dermal tissue still present brushing against the sweater I hung over my shoulders to disguise the gaping shotgun wound I sustained to become a zombie, which I do not want to talk about - not over just one corpse.

Walking out in such a way as to look as if one were walking around, we stumbled upon a piece, completely unrelated to the opening, that we both enjoyed with the delighted surprise of also finding another who appreciated the so-called: "Human Rights Art". It was a child's watercolor of a cut stem flower, two dimensional but still representing a sense of achievement: Something to be striven towards; a certain Stillness, despite being a representation of living death.

Lo and behold, fate intervened in our favor as we stumbled - right outside of the freaking Gallery - into a "food truck", i.e. a truck filled with humans who were somehow, yet again, unaware, did not hear doom shambling up behind them and: ...

"Brains!" we said together, enjoying the sense of balance one may feel when meeting someone whom one actually wanted to meet, maybe had dreamed about a little even. "Brains." I reminded her afterward.

What strange habits remain with us: we spent an

hour trying to find a place for her to brush

the ground lumps which were once her teeth.

Yes, it was a weirdly neurotic exercise but I

was so entranced that I could not help but

follow, despite the paths being

unintentionally listless and zig-zagging.

"Brains - brains." I love to hear her words

tinged with the tone of laughter; I think of

how she must have looked upon first dying:

how fresh and vigorous her decaying mass

must have appeared, looming up and over

the ridge at a KOA or State Park campsite:

tearing through entrails with the glee of a

little girl popping bubbles.

One each of either potential-partner's hands, each missing several finger joints, found one another before the Sun's romantically hellish glare cleared to descend into the darkness.

Some gristly pops and we both slowed before the disparity in our motion and directions would tear our clasped hands from their arms or worse the arms from our bodies; after all of that effort and upon getting to a suitable space to brush her teeth it is discovered that her purse was left at the food truck earlier and we then turned-the-fleet to head back in that direction, without disconnecting and she feels a little awkward for dragging me around the Industrial Art District in ever-increasingly narrow, concentric, quixotic, circles: but, honestly, there was no better place to be but by her side, now that I was there with the best of my post-life articulatory powers, I turned to her, gurgling: "Brains." and I knew she understood.

II: iv a

An asymmetrical plane of midnight black hair

again fell across the side of her face and the

sighed pierce the otherwise steady sound of

liquid being slipped through straws with the

occasional - although always faint -

reminder that a health club was but a

soundproof wall away.

"Oh, I don't know..." is said to the woman with

stylishly short blonde hair that precipiently

started to wave upward right where the road

bike helmet would stop.

"What don't you know?" Hand to corner of mouth to catch the conversationally loosened beverage remnant then trying to find a better path of least resistance onto her clothing.

"Oh you know ... The usual... Everything." A laugh and the hair pushed impatiently behind a shapely ear; "In particular, that I have thought a lot about me and the Drac lately: constantly - trying to get a fix on what is next."

"Are y'all all-right?"

The black-haired, alabaster-skinned woman exhaled so completely that her yoga uniform seem to deflate on itself.

"I just do not know."

"Oh - Kathy - I'm sorry... " and words failing,
     her hand gently came to rest upon that of the
     dark-haired woman -with indelible
     femininity- so as to facilitate a positive flood
     of feelings: positive and reassuring.

The hand now occupied, the ear defying hair is
     thus policed by futile - but fun! - puffs of
     breath from her mouth's corner - after one
     such puff: a weak smile.

"Thanks - I really don't have many people to talk
     to about this..."

"Who does? - the let me ask you right away (her
eyes narrowing and adjusting focus so as to
overtly peer into the soul of her old friend)
"Is it the hunting? Is it still fun?"

"Truthfully (the yoga clothes balloon deflates now
completely) it has become dull and
mechanical. The satisfaction of habit -
instead of the satiation of desire. It is evident
from the fiery yellow-red glow in his eyes
that his thoughts are elsewhere; and that's
not the root of the problem but a
symptom..."

"What do you mean?"

"Well - for the past... God: really? 150 years I
have thought there was some distance, but

lately - its been palpable; even when he is
present he is absent. Does that make any
sense?"

A knowing smile and warmly squinted eyes, a
        gentle increase of the supporting downward
        pressure exerted from the Top Hand.

"More than you know... Vlad and I - oh, back
        around the start of the Industrial Revolution,
        were bored also, but we did what lots of
        couples did then... "

" Have affairs?"

"No - We buried our pain below the level of
        perceptible outward expression and

soldiered on, the envy of our friends and
foes alike."

"But y'all look so happy."

" Oh and we are! That was quite some time ago
and we have implemented a variety of
compensatory strategies recommended by
Dr. Irene Cassorla which I will share with
you later. I have one of her books in the car.
Nonetheless, Blue Skies, if perennial, do
also oppress and although I live a life of
perennially firm gender-specific physical
accessories and have not had a cold in 1,000
years: a sly smile: "...We even have the
matching, connectable, His and Hers coffins,
as featured in the brochure of *The Stereotype
for the Happy Couple*, but yet, I also worry -

too - that I missed something; I knew what I
     never knew way back when and the image
     represent is little but the facade that strains
     to hold back the truth; the pills help by the
     way. "

They both laugh and the starry eyes of the blonde
     friend also serve to conduct warmth across
     the table. She begins again:

"But you must be a dancing queen, if you dance
     away from my questions as adroitly as you
     have so proven: Are you fulfilled as a
     woman and a vampire?"

Tears well up and the recalcitrantly-obstinate wall
     of hair served as convenient curtain behind

which eyes were rubbed and nose dabbed with napkin.

"There's something about the way he looks at the maid, the new one... "

"That Werewolf bitch!"

"In her defense, it's not her fault, so much: being young and that attractive is not her fault; but I suspect she may enjoy the extra smidge of attention that she receives for Tarting it up a few percentage points or so."

A gasp, a pregnant pause, and then: "Oh God."

"What is it? "

" It's got to be a coincidence but I have noticed an

    unusual preponderance of hair clogs in the

    shower, as of late."

" ...You can stay with us if you want."

"I wonder what your Dr. Cassorla has to say about

    it? Shall we see over a post-workout

    cigarette in the car?"

"But they are so bad for one."

"Sometimes - however - the most healthy option

    is presented by the least healthy

    opportunity."

II: iv b

Weeks Later, the roles - somewhat changed, to that end, in fact, reversed as Anneane-Anthia: the blonde, was disconnected and spacey, whereas Kathy, up from the previous Low's, noticed this and approach the problem in her own style.

"Vamnav or something? Ordinarily you have appraised the purchase and resale value of several of the posteriors in this room, but - strangely, today: no figures are being quoted to me aloud."

Her hair, still very short and still, very blond,

shifted a little in the enforced air current of

the post workout Synth Blood bar; she takes

a long and very intentional drag on the dark

red smoothie - diet, of course - and she

pauses to watch bubbles float up in the

plastic-glasses bottom. A sigh into a posture

reappraisal, a mirror check assisted curve

placement review and adjustment wiggle

and as she smoothed her yoga trousers of

lines, invisible and real, she spoke:

"Ya' got me; I'm all hung up on some family

drama and now, just with you saying that, it

Dawns on me that there is an existential toll,

too."

"Did someone bite someone that they should not
have?"

"Christ" - a laugh - "I wish it was that prosaic - I
had to move my grandmother into one of
those homes for elderly immortals; it's been
over the past two weeks; she has - to put it
politely- declining cognitive faculties, with
the last 500 years being the epicenter of her
confusion; and now, Me: I cannot seem to
focus on anything, either."

Anneane-Anthia nods in assent, continuing:

"And the thing is, that it can happen to any of us;
we think Grandma went off the synth blood
on vacation in the UK during that big
Jakob-Creutzfeldt outburst and who even

believed in Prions, then, - except for that one scientist who was reviled for saying "Hey I found out something y'all should look at regarding virus fragments: and even he who knew anyway that prions could even, in our most remote and self-loathing dreams, affect the undead with the population destabilizing efficacy?"

"Oh I think I read about that next to the sex tips in Demono- Cosmopolitan-Flex, its because they appear to result from viral shattering, right? So that their effects therefore become unpredictable, correct?"

"As if British food could be any worse!?!"

"Demono- Cosmopolitan-Flex also said that it was

probably a vampire government plot to kill

vampires but that does not make any sense

because there are only a handful of vampires

who are not affiliated with the various

governmental services, anyway, so it would

be a largely self-destructive act, which

suggests - her her own black-blue hair

behaving today, thanks to the help of a

silicone impregnated headband: "Oh God,

maybe if that is true, it's the negative

impression of vampires in the media that are

causing vampires to construct elaborate

fantasy situations that result in their own

mass extinction via: suicide."

"You would really like my grandmother, would

you mind visiting her a little bit and

pretending that you were me?"

"Are you asking that - seriously?"

"At first... no, but now that you ask..."

"Sure if nothing else is going on and you really

need it."

II: v

To best direct artificially intelligenced robots to

direct themselves, Pleasure and Pain were

introduced into their programming via the

so-called: "Sex Drive" providing, thusly,

the conative force of a physical reward in

accomplishing goals. Incidentally, several

types of robot consumable drugs were

explored, in-trial, but the results turned the

stomach of the most grizzled of researchers,

still, even today, robot ready drugs, never

publicly revealed therefore well-known

amongst the public, the clandestine manufacture and distribution facilitated by an ever-growing number of humans - always eager for profit - and a few more-shadowy corners hosted the nightly ministations of less scrupulous providers of the robotic persuasion.

Combining the two topics we have a fresh, vibrantly young -maybe like six months after manufacturing (e.g 28 in human maturity) - and charmingly fetching couple, safely sexually active, walking away from said corner with secret compartments filled with the - just to make it easier for humans - "Robot Marijuana" they preferred to recreationally consume in the stead of petroleum-based beverages, which were as unhealthy as they are legal.

We find the couple at home, lying in post

     Robo-Coital repose, tenderly sharing a

     robot-joint and debriefing re: their

     love-making; it had proven to be enjoyable

     to both, but she had a question repeatedly

     presenting itself to her awareness throughout

     the session so, now, a little high and

     neon-glowing she asked, with no small

     temerity:

"So what... Do you ever maybe think about

     swapping our genital components, since they

     are modular, and make love like that?"

"Hard-Nope."

Exhaling smoke, in a manner so as to feign frustration, she began the process of Pretty Persuasion* (*Shameless REM reference).

"But why? It's not as if the switch would hurt; there are numerous articles attesting, even, that the mutual loosening and then Re-Screwing of our respective G-Bolts may prove quite pleasurable."

Exhaling smoke, repeatedly, he already knew he was beat. The outcome being so apparent that he accepted it as is as inevitable; but maybe he could stall... She continued:

"It's not, like, temporarily installing my genitalia reduces your stature or credibility as a manbot; this won't shake loose any latent

homosexual aspect of your personality; I just
want to share the sensation of me, having
you, in you, so as to most effectively
articulate how satisfying and pleasurable
Robo-Sex with you always is."

"It's not that, but - really - I have only had
    mechanical failures when trying to access
    my male G-Bolt. It is definitely not as easy
    as that sample issue of Cosmos said;
    anyway: I've done some research…"

"That is great, as it implies a healthy curiosity and
    only low-powered inhibition circuits on your
    behalf."

"Would you like me to strip, too? Do a little dance
    perhaps?"

The joint reduced to embers, little else glowed in the charged-darkness, besides their cooly glowing and warmly illuminating, system status lights. Crushing out the stub she, post checkmate, sweetly asked him to roll another while she began to seek out the uniquely shaped G-Bolt socket and wrench; then adding: "You know, I have no idea what shall cause my first erection ever, but I am glad that it's you."

II: vi

In the candle's light, she could not differentiate Iris

Brown from Pupil Black and as she tried, it

proved impossible to avoid ascribing to the

speaker, a known and generally considered:

"Gallivantingly Chivalrous" style of

Time-Traveler, a credibility proportionate to

the clarity lost to clear thinking, as the cost

of thought itself.

So, when he said: "So despite the appearance of

　　　our relationship being longer in duration

　　　than the average, I must admit..."

The waiter arrives with their soup. Hers: just right;

　　　his: too hot. He continues thusly:

" ... That conception is more properly conceived

　　　as an illusion based on a falsely processed

　　　and subsequently, incorrectly experienced,

　　　modality of space-time existenz which - and

　　　please do not let this upset your apparently

　　　delicious soup- but for technical reasons

　　　beyond the course of this meal, I

　　　experienced this -our- "We" more quickly

　　　than yourself and will thus age less quickly

　　　at a proportionate rate and so if you see me

with other girls in the past or future: that's
totally why."

Bending to his soup as she rose from her own, a
quizzical expression begins to form but is
marred somewhat by strand of something,
half submerged in soup, half attached to her
lip; only condensation graced the silver ice
bin as it arced beautifully through the air: up
and across the room and descending -all but
in slow motion- to whiz by his head such
that it was later said: hot soup saved him
from deep shit: as a man - apparently the
twin of the male member of this couple of,
but with a dashing eye patch and a
world-weary expression, linearly charged
across the quadratic space in attempt to
parabolically uplift he of the recently

acquired soup but lost in a reverie of
expletives directed at the (but shouted):
"Dolt who was about to ruin it with the best
girl, in-all time that he shall ever meet and at
the rest of his life afterwards would be
scorched Wasteland of existential loneliness,
where he - not willing to die - chasing the
dragon of lost love - instead barely lives."

She gently chides herself for having intentionally
forgotten a well-established personal
stricture: "Don't eat hash cakes while or
before going out on dates." and excuses
herself to the restroom while an assistant
manager does his best to spatula his arms
between the two versions of the same man; a
hostess places a piece of paper, ostensibly
with a communication number of some sort,

into the pocket of the younger of the two men, being identical beings, as it were, he of the double eye. Shrieking further, he of the eyepatch fainted dead away just after having muttered a statement that "Destiny really is irreparable."

For in that wintry moment of sincere discontent, a flash freeze disambulated his Souls: if no one arrives to help from the future, to help the person from the future, is it that the future person dies before he finished his living in this time?

<h1 style="text-align:center">II: vii</h1>

Fall fell upon a College Town atop the most

    mysterious of the Cascade Mountain

    Summits; also in descendence: the Annual

    Homecoming events, large and small;

    actions: symbolic, figurative, and/or literal.

Combining the conflictingly harmonic aspects of

    all three aforementioned categorization

    forms - the substantially stoned sophomore

    Sasquatch son narrated, to himself, ever

    onward in which our protagonist -him, me -

introduces his glamorous "Long-Term" - of
two months - girlfriend to his
lower-medium level donor parents in an
overfilled, understaffed, "take your parents
to" type restaurant so as to best elicit and
subsequently enjoy their reaction from
meeting a modern female Sasquatch who
waxes: all over.

"Aren't you cold, dear - just a little cold?" His
mother's girlfriend directed words drew him
out in time to see his father's eyes cloud with
the self-recrimination and chastisement
precipitately resultant - unquestionably -
from a too-languorous look upon his own
son's lover. Thus, his plan to prevent being
"cut off" by embarrassing his parents so
thoroughly at the time of intended

exposition of the thought of being "cut-off"
that all thoughts, whether proximal or distal
to the possibility of being "cut-off" therefore
become permanently precluded.

Phase 2: the injection of non sequiturs whose
meaning - obtuse at first- then unfolds with
the subtlety of a cluster munition over a
grade school with each passing moment of
the ideas existence being in thought:

"So I bought these almonds the other day at the
abortion clinic but as I was not hungry, I
started to hide them places, instead. "

"We were asked to babysit her sisters toddler - all
the time... - until he ended up in the pound."

The entree's detritus swept aside - now, sometime

later, coffee being poured for dessert: the

mother politely asks for and then received,

graciously, a container of cream from the

utterly depilated undergraduate debutante;

only to find: a hair floating within.

Nearly assured funding for at least another

semester, soon appeared before him; the

same time as vapor from a surreptitiously hit

hash pen, itself emanating outward from

him, exited with a final non-sequitur, itself a

contradiction to the others; eye's never

leaving those of either parent:

Referring to his girlfriend: "Before we got

together I was - small world, eh? - saying:

'Bye Bye to Bi-Curious and replacing it

with Good Day: Gay!' Because of our

current waiters -... Uh... - wine opening

technique; but then he left me for a

cardboard cutout of himself - but in leather

- which in turn shocked me straight into the

arms of my baby over here: his befurred

pointing digit aimed directly at the

potted-plant next to his girlfriend.

II: iix

My Dearest,

Although your capacity to grasp this letter is

somewhat truncated by your limited,

although always winsome, verbal processing

capacities, please know that although

printed, you shall first know of these words

from my own mouth.

New relationships - such as the one we find

ourselves experiencing now - when

successful, are filled with Rainbows, Sunshine, Farts consisting of vanilla ice cream and every other concept ground into dusty familiarity within our modern purview and experienced by the blood driven greeting card Gristmill. And I mean that in a good way.

New relationships also present the opportunity to expose the nascent, burgeoning couple, to the strain of awkwardness since, even with CIA agents, Androids and Corpses, the Specter of spirits of relationships past float always into new relationships, and as a universe wide rule, shall always occur at the worst possible time. Not wishing to spend any moment of my the precious present of the present with you, I hereby write this letter as a way of alluding, however obtusely, to the murky depths of my

affection for you by sharing some of the

details for my previous relationships. In this

sense we can exercise any demons, be they

actual, hypothetical, presumed, projected, or

possibly revealed during a rerun of a cop

chase show, which, incidentally, is how my

father proposed to my mother; not marriage,

mind you, but he proposed to knock her up

while being handcuffed and beaten on the

hood of her - she then being a stranger - car

hood. How she honked and honked hoping

to somehow stem the tide of paint

destroying blood flowing from his face and

fashionable, self-imposed, Stigmata. Also,

that this was the third time this week

L.E.O's used the hood of her super compact

car as a bludgeon, bedecked with peace

signs and stickers advocating for increased communication and loving one's enemies; moreover: she was already late for work.

She, although a remarkably attractive pharmacist, had proven largely unboyfriendable and the increasingly incoherent protestation of instant love screamed through the reddening glass of the windscreen, was the most romantic request she had known since her college boyfriend suggested banal sex. Ostensibly as a witness, she accompanied him to the emergency room and after contriving a collision, squeezed his hand and whispered quickly that he should look for an emergency exit after being left in triage because she would arrange a: "... d vowel sounds."

He thought, did she say distraction or or

destruction? Possibly: " d e s c i s o c o "

if she speaks a little Latin. But, as he was

placed onto the exam table, she first tripped

over a wet floor sign, forcing a finger down

her throat, causing a profuse explosion of

vomit and then, coming up tore off her top

to reveal a stained and masonically

emblemed Sports Bra, it's elastic betraying

the same symptoms it was created an

employed to prevent from happening to her

own body. As the simultaneously hilarious,

disgusting, and erotic moment of time

temporarily unwitted the delicate L.E.O.'s

he took off and she shrieked, pointing in

orthogonal direction: "Look: an alien

dressed as an illegal alien!" and then herself

took-off for an exit. Thankfully, because of a tragic parade accident, many members of the attractive, but secretive, Shriner Late-Twenties - which reportedly has reached 65 in some people - women's volleyball team had suffered a strange altogether unheard-of, synchronized parade accident where those men, a few of whom infarcting cardiacly in consequence of having young breasts, despite being squished themselves, after having been squished against them; just too hot. But - I realize I am rambling. One last thing, mom had found that Sports Bra at her house after a party and decided to keep it. She never even played ball with the Shriners.

I point this out because as she was walking out a

ritualistically aproned and sports bra-ed

woman pointing up from the crowd, in

confusion that she was being stripped by the

hospital in preparation for their sacrifice of

her, since she was the only virgin of the

group. Dead Silence: both men and women

Snicker; in vain attempt to quiet the Snicker

it explodes into a guffaw which is even

joined by the otherwise stone-faced doctors,

culminating in her own Trip, Barf, Flash

into escape combo again; incidentally this

technique is yet to ever be improved upon.

Thus explained: my humble roots.

What I am working towards, however, in

highlighting the unnatural pairing of my

forebears, seeks to cushion the next

Revelation. As an adult, I have, sexually, identified with those who seek to procreate with robots. Not like, by any means, fancy expensive BhangBots and their 300 RPM swivel-hip motors; but instead, and this shows the power of love to uplift and equalize, as in our case: the love of a man and his self guided: fuzzy logic guided, self-driven vacuum cleaner.

And is it so surprising, my dear ##45acds (this is what we humans call a nickname and I gave you this one because it implies, inherently, you are a sexy bitch: in or out of the circular French maid costume I purchased for you at Halloween last year) that I fell for you, who, single-handedly solve my Dust Bunny infestation and ended the drifts of animal hair which had persisted despite the presence of no animals. You - who charge yourself with the grace and dignity displayed by Royal, self-guided, vacuuming units; you who can empty her own bin, thank you; you: who has felt like a "She" from the first moments of removing "Her" OEM plastic and styrofoams.

II: ix

Turning in her chair to directly face the therapist,
the female shape-shifter confesses, in
response to a query about her therapeutic
goals: "I just want to look into the mirror
and like who and what I see." Covering for
this moment of vulnerability, she continued:
" ... Or maybe I have it backwards and the
truly uncomfortable situation is being stared
at and via projection, judged: by my own
reflection, who I do not recognize. Peering
back into me with the exact force exerted to
peer into her: looking for something familiar

- but lost; which upon contact with then yield a positive aspect on my behalf to her and therefore she to me... "

"What is it that you are looking for?"

"Self-acceptance."

"Hmmm. Now you mentioned earlier that you are, by birth and by semi-divine decree, a shapeshifter capable of assuming any human visage, correct? "

"Yes" is said in the same exhalation as a sigh of boredom.

" ... And this ability - gift - provides no relief from the distaste you feel with how you look?"

"I said: 'who' and 'what'... Stared back', earlier, remember? "

The therapist nods in assent and her client

continues: "...Never once; and I used to try

- really!- assuming every form I could think

of - from classical-serf to Elvis

Impersonator with no combination

producing such a creation that I could meet

the look of my own eyes cooley, letting the

details come to me instead of the smash and

dash of the anxious burst of attention

remedied by an aversion of the eyes."

"Have you considered that your inability to look at

yourself in the eyes as being similar - at

least in terms of the metaphor, to one not

being able to see into themselves thereby

preventing or precluding the identification

with themselves and unification with this
vital aspect of the self?"

A look of delight on her face; "Ha! Right there,
now that: is worth the co-pay!"

II: x

Sleep came in ever shortening fits and bursts with

    the intervals in-between ever, always,

    growing larger. Too hot to be too cold, too

    comfortable to be constricted: too much

    in-love to feel annoyed, I did my best to

    thrash into a more comfortable position so

    as to assist in the passing of the Blue-Black

    Morning Light but the covers seem stapled

    to the mattress and all eight of her tentacles

fully circumscribed the entirety of my
corporeal being.

Hungry, needing to use the restroom, the
involuntary recollection of a co-worker's
seductive and seemingly-sincere display of
color changes did little to distract away from
the Neon-Bright realization that despite the
reach and power of her embrace, the
attribute desired to be contained therein -
this primitive and decentralized circulatory
system - pulsed uninhibited within him. It
did not pulse with her name or it's Morse
Code synonym.

II: xi

And looking up from the calculations, his own and

already double-checked, the solution

remained inviolate and conclusive: Love.

At least - he thought while blowing a strand

of hair away from the field of his vision -

At least the result would suggest the

possibility of a relationship between the

matrices of their lives, the arrays of their

feelings, and therefore their Trend towards

Unity - possibly identity - as found in the

constituent coordinates of the known

orthogonal - touchingly - moments of exclusively unjust suffering in either life.

Dawn's orange glow led to Wagnerian yellows: the shift in spectrum continuously proving the reliability of the S.A.S. results and therefore his own validity as a programmer and competency as a statistical theoretician. It indeed was almost certainly, probably, Love - he thought - smoke trailing from the carelessly adored cigarette, and a laugh of Delight and Dread: of life itself - accompanied his high pressure sodium illuminated footfalls, several days later.

The calculations themselves called upon a subtle understanding of: Bohr's Complementarity; Heisenberg's Uncertainty, and the somewhat controversial and exceedingly awkward code contribution from Schrodinger's appeal to Vendantic teaching. Green chili salsa falls upon these sections of the code from the beautifully overstuffed, two-aluminum foil, spliff-type rolled burrito.

The results again obtained, upon further replication, later that day, at duck pond. The gray plane of the Desert Horizon lept to embrace the blue, blue electric blue, sky which contains, but does not permeate the obsidian sheet of the Duck's aqueous environs.

The joint of $40 an ounce swag weed threw a runner, despite the paper's infused-saliva insulation; the same situation that he himself was in - if, hypothetically, a mallard duck's research went directly and uniformly askew and then years after he quacks at the fading reflection of a particular duck that quantum theory, itself understood only through painfully derived multivariate linear equations representing metric-fucktons of immaculately yielded row points to the right of the decimal data points which proceed to conclusively, yet again, suggest that they were meant for one another with an alpha equaling .005 notwithstanding.

II: xii

The two bluish-gray conglomerates of ghostly mist

floated down the Twilight lit sidewalk

slightly too far away from one another to

interconnect, but Much Too Close for mere

acquaintanceship; of the sunset, approaching

traffic, and even their own destination: they

knew nothing, so wrapped in being rapt

were they.

Sampling, as a result of the extrapolation from the

specific to the general, inherently

contributes error to a statistical measure; this

must be kept in mind as we now direct our

attention to a merely fractional-fragment of

the unfolding fractals of this couple's

affection.

Looking down toward, but always up to, his

hoped-for significant other, the ostensibly

masculine component of the couple asked,

all but to the air between them: "What do

you think about death after life?"

A sigh to release an exhalation; an exhalation

sounding like a sigh: "Jesus - what's your

hang-up with physics when you know

perfectly well that our own existence is all

but perfectly circumscribed by
metaphysics?"

Something seems to soften the unintentionally
sharp rejoinder; this something thereafter
arrests his forward-floating such that a
moment is spent paying heed to how
flattering the Blue Hour is to her
agglomerated mass.

The time spent smiling toward her transmuted into
time having lived, alive.

Catching up at a crosswalk, she looked before
hesitating to cross; without looking, her
face-analog whirled completely around to
face him: kind of sweaty, unambiguously
out of breath, still enraptured by the

entire-totality-of-the-ever-fleeting-moment:
he - impressed and puffed up with himself,
shared these insights with she of whose
molecules he longed to entangle his own
within.

"How high are you?"

Not at all akin the questions he had already
rehearsed answering, he nonetheless replied
with a surprised honesty: "A little."

"Yeah - you are not making a lot of sense back
there."

That something then again struck him, forcing the
outward display of a grin so goofy it bore
absolutely zero resemblance to the

solemnity owed to the framing of her pretty

visage by the evening's first few stars. If

only there were hands to hold that which

would be her face!

Or, finally, a two-block delayed Snappy Remark:

"We need the Physical World or at least its

concept, false as it is, maybe - to completely

accentuate our experience of the

Metaphysical World.

In those moments where he lagged behind, she

took time to ponder, via rhetorical statement

conveyed *sotto voce*: "How odd he is, being

so friendly - even at the best of her worst."

She floated closer for being farther away, seeing

him as cute beneath the sodium glow of the

streetlamp. Deeply physical fears rumbled
within her metaphysical innards; unused to
the sensation, she paid little mind to the
corresponding sense of nagging-dread
inarticulately howling warnings from
another realm - like from a human story - to
unlistening ears in this one.

II: xiii

Morning arrives too early, the bar's darkness: too

    bright. They who had - the night before -

    doffed business attire to don the fur of

    lycanthropy nevertheless drifted in, naked

    and alone.

Two such wolf-men, now man-wolves, sat slackly

    at a cluttered table; their silence itself

    screaming re: the severity of the hangover's

    that both, generally quite staid, fellows

lingered lumberingly within, each assuming
the dull visage of those trapped beneath
earthquake rubble; not noticing the various
twigs and fence accoutrements that adorned
the wounds, freshly acquired, and slowly
healing back to the normal level of slightly
better-than-average, the unique and
generally involuntarily contracted illness
liberates with: "Without".

Origin undetermined: a statement appears in the
space between the two as an echo of
resonant sentiment of remarks both and
made, so often before - Spoken- and Un- -
"It really hurts my feelings, when, you
know, it's a full moon and I'm starting my
cycle and something completely normal

happens, causing my wife to snippily ask:
'Is it that time of the month'?"

Coffee and bathrobes are delivered to the
gentleman at this point; The Establishment
in which they found themselves being a
werewolf bar, itself named: "Hairballs",
catered to such special-needs customers and
already had credit cards on file for they who
did not think to grab a wallet on their way
out to shred raw animals into muzzle sized
portions.

The slightly older, apparently, of the Two Men
followed: "Tell me about it; right, like, I'm
(expletive deleted)bald and yet I am still
being blamed when the shower drain is
clogged with hair; or when a hoof gets left

in the toilet, accidentally. I shouldn't have to
apologize for my biological functioning."

The younger, leaning forward, as being newly
married he still enjoyed complaining about
his wife: "It's all projection you know; my
wife sees me change and shift into a
More-Alive Being, if but once a month: I go
to prowl, I go to consume, I go to the wild;
she resents me for having to stay at home -
we have some Pupps, you know - and
although she did couch the whole:
"Home-Dungeon" idea in sexy terms - she
focused on the decorating and not on the
hardware and those restraints tore off like a
cotton-candy-condom the moment
Moonlight hit the window; think of that: she
chose the dungeon for the Moonlight View;

I love her, but Christ, shouldn't they come with warning labels that are apparent the day before the day after the honeymoon?"

The older man chuckles softly before saying: "Don't worry it only gets worse. But there shall be no factory recalls on defective parts, or no complimentary service: each marriage is largely D.I.Y. And the instruction manual was written in an agglutinative language."

"Oh, please do not get me started. I understand that blood is hard to remove from tile, I get that, but - and I was very clear about this before marriage - if I have transformed into a state in which I have paws, instead of hands, not to mention an overwhelming bloodlust that desires to be slaked - mopping is less than

224

on my agenda. She made this crack, about
getting fixtures which service dogs are able
to actuate. In my head I was like: female
dog: heal! I did not ask to be this way and
God Don't Make Junk."

"But you did not say that right?"

"Oh (expletive deleted) no, I went through the
     hassle of getting married, why would I want
     to end it like that?"

Sipping his coffee, his hangover temporarily
     precluded by the nostalgic images parading
     before his Mind's Eye: "Don't worry son, as
     it gets worse, and it shall, it will become
     better, in a sense."